This Walker book belongs to:

_____

_____

_____

snare

bass drum

pedal

drumsticks

chimes

tom-tom

floor tom

cowbell

brushes

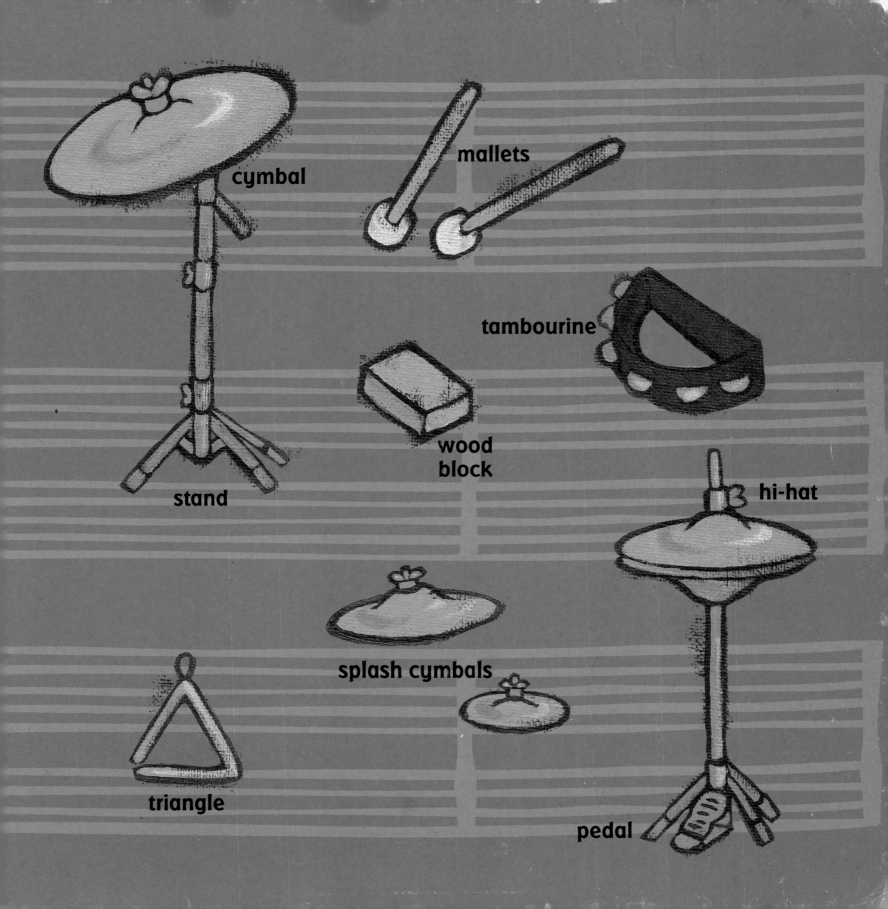

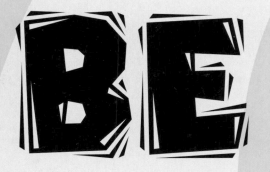

BE QUIET,

**To Jason and Beck for the loud inspiration,
and Gram and Gramps for making sure everyone wears ear protection!**

First published 2011 by Walker Books Ltd, 87 Vauxhall Walk, London SE11 5HJ • 2 4 6 8 10 9 7 5 3 1 • Copyright © 2011 Leslie Patricelli • The right of Leslie Patricelli to be identified as author/illustrator of this work has been asserted by her in accordance with the Copyright, Designs and Patents Act 1988 • This book has been typeset in Badger • Printed in China • All rights reserved • No part of this book may be reproduced, transmitted or stored in an information retrieval system in any form or by any means, graphic, electronic or mechanical, including photocopying, taping and recording, without prior written permission from the publisher • British Cataloguing-in-Publication Data: a catalogue record for this book is available from the British Library • ISBN 978-1-4063-3650-4 • www.walker.co.uk

MIKE!

SLAP

Thwack

klunk

LESLIE PATRICELLI

WALKER BOOKS
AND SUBSIDIARIES
LONDON · BOSTON · SYDNEY · AUCKLAND

This is a story about a monkey named Mike,
who started drumming as a tiny little tyke.

He played with his fingers,
he played with his feet –
a funky little monkey with a

beat, beat, beat.

**Bing, bong, bing,
his rhythms would sing,**

but poor Monkey Mike
heard only one thing…

He heard it from his parents,
he heard it from his sis,
he heard it from the neighbours
and it sounded like this:

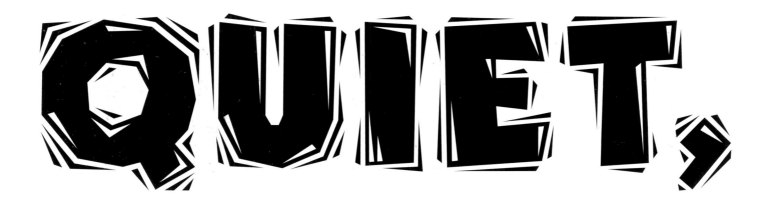

His mum and dad had hope
that he'd stop as he got older,
but as Mike grew bigger
his rhythms just got bolder!

He played on the table
like a wild baboon.

He played on the dolls
in his little sister's room.

TONK

But everywhere he played,
he heard the same tune:

Mike tried to be quiet,
he tried to be still,
but the beat of his heart
was stronger than his will.

Mike was good at school –
he wasn't one for yapping,
but with pencils everywhere
he couldn't stop tapping.

No noise was the rule
all day long.
And every single day,
he heard that same old song …

Then one day, Mike was walking with his dad
when he saw in a window a hairy young lad
beating on a red thing
that shone like a jet –

a real live, full-size

jamming drum set!

And there at the drum set,
an ape with long fur,
beating so fast –
arms and legs a blur.

He boomed on a bass drum,
rolled on a snare,
banged on a floor tom,
sticks in the air.

BOOM CHICK, BOOM CHICK, ZAT ZOOM CRASH!
HI-HAT, HI-HAT, BASS, TOM SMASH!

tap
tap

Mike's heart was in pieces;
he couldn't deny it.
He wanted that set
and he just couldn't buy it.

ting
bing

But that *want* got him dreaming...
That *need* made him think...

AHA!
An idea! It arrived in a blink.

Mike took out his sketch pad
and started to draw.
His mind had a picture;
he sketched what he saw.

Then he *really* got to work –
his room was a disaster!
He ripped tape, clanged metal,
faster and faster.

HAMMER BANG, HAMMER BANG, DING BOOM BAM
RIP-TAPE, RIP-TAPE, TIE GLUE WHAM!

When Mike had finished,
he sat down on his throne,
twirled his sticks and …

made a sound all his own!

DIGGETY DIGGETY

ZAT ZOOM CRASH!

COFFEE CAN

COFFEE CAN

POT PAN SPLASH!

He rolled on his bucket,
rang on his chimes,
pulled out his bananas
and played in double time!

Mike played so hard,
he fell off his seat –
but even on the floor,
he never missed a beat!

First chimes, then a fill,
and a BOOM, BOOM, swish!
Then he looked up in surprise…

It was his mum, dad and sis!

His mum started clapping!
Then his dad, then his sis!
They hooted and they cheered
and they blew him a kiss!

And do you know what they said?
Well, it sounded like this…

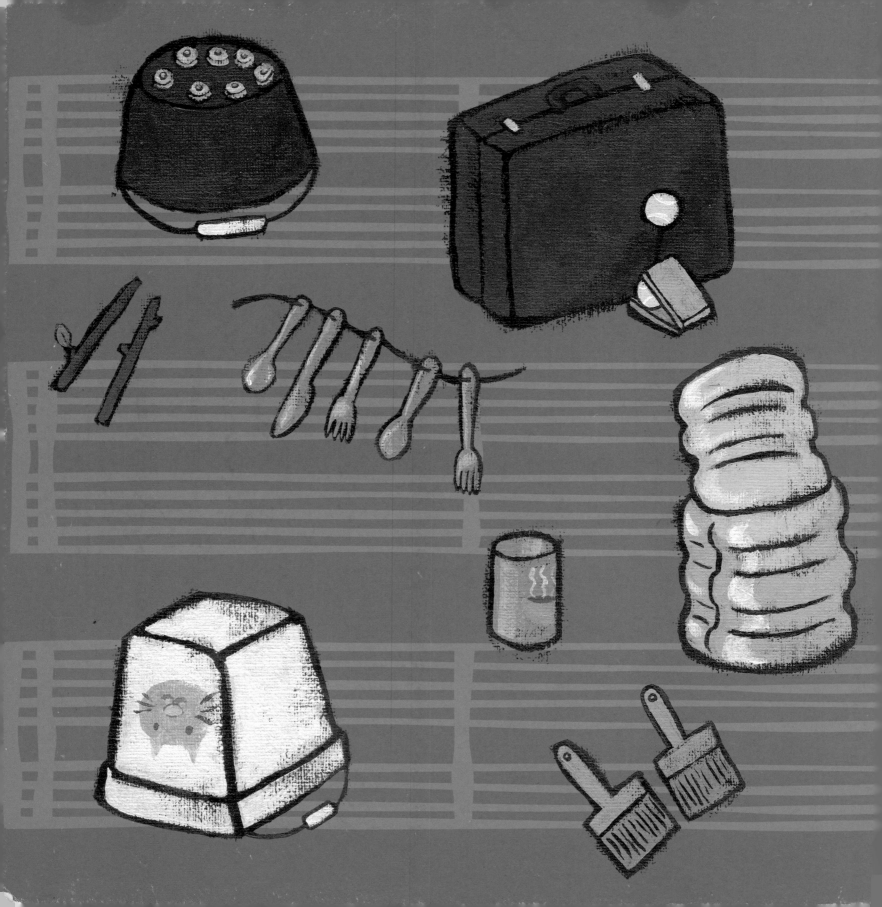

Another title by Leslie Patricelli

ISBN 978-1-4063-2244-6

Available from all good bookstores

www.walker.co.uk